To: Becky!

Thanks for being a vne.

[signature]

Maury C. Moose
and
The Facebrook

Maury C. Moose
and
The Facebrook

by
Adam
Baker

Illustrated by Jennifer Marshall

Maury C. Moose
and The Facebrook

Published in Arizona by Stapled By Mom Publishing.

ISBN 978-0996719001 paperback
ISBN 978-0996719018 eBook

To my grandparents. The only thing more fun than writing this book was getting to share its progress with you.

~ Adam

To my loving family and friends - and to THAT moose at the Alaska Zoo. You know who you are.

Love,
Jen

Introduction

When we last heard from
Maury and the gang,
their plan to save Christmas
ended with a bang.
They got rid of G.R. Inchworm
and the forest was saved.
The story was told around town
and the audience raved.
But what does a Christmas-loving forest
do in the spring?
Sit back and wait to see
what the next adventure will bring.
There's always another tale to be told
and a lesson to learn.
To find out what happens,
the next page you should turn!

Chapter 1

Every kid dreams of being a hero, and Maury C. Moose was no different. Movies, books and TV shows are filled with unexpected heroes who, against all odds, defeat the bad guy. The feeling of saving the day has to be one of the greatest feelings ever, but there is another feeling that comes with any heroic act.

Every great hero knows this feeling too and Maury C. Moose was no different.

Maury was happy to have saved Christmas for Forest Noel. He appreciated the smiles and well wishes from folks around town, but now he was experiencing the forgotten part of every hero's journey. The one that is left out of the superhero movies.

Maury didn't expect the feeling of exhaustion that comes with being a celebrity. The constant attention from the press. The requests for interviews, autographs and selfies.

All great heroes have gone through it. Harry Otter had to wear contact lenses and a fake mustache to avoid the paparazzi after he saved Frogwarts. Rocky Bal Boa Constrictor became so tired of constantly being asked to slither up those famous stairs that he faked a back injury.

The attention is great at first, but it can wear on even the super-est of heroes.

Maury now knew this feeling all too well. After word had gotten out about how he and his friends had magically revitalized Jingle Bell Block, Forest Noel was a hub of constant activity. Maury could hardly leave his house without being swarmed to recount the story of how they ran G.R. Inchworm out of town. Daily, he was mobbed by adoring fans.

And that doesn't even include all the press. One morning he was on the cover of the Hoofington Post. The next day he had a feature story on Good Morning Forest Noel. Later, he was asked to read the Top 10 list on the Stephen Col Bear show. ESPN Newts even created a 30-for-30 documentary of his daring Christmas adventure.

Everyone wanted to hear the story of how a group of young students was able to clean up all the trash in the forest in just one night. Mikey Duck, Simon C.

Owl, Page Ant, Justine Beaver, Stoc King Crab, Julia, and Rob Birds all had their 15 minutes of fame, but most of the focus fell squarely on the antlers of the one hero with the merriest name of all time…*Maury Chris Moose*!

The hero who saved Christmas even had a name that sounded like the words "Merry Christmas." No wonder the media couldn't get enough.

T-shirts, bumper stickers and Christmas cards were created featuring the phrase "Maury ChrisMoose!" Sales of Beets headphones, the ones used to cover up G.R. Inchworm's hearing, soared and everyone wanted to take a picture with the new car air freshener Mikey had used to make Jingle Bell Block smell so fresh and so clean.

Maury was happy to have saved the forest and prevented the construction of the Bar Hum Bug, but he was ready for things to settle down. He couldn't wait for a new story to make its way into town and take Forest Noel's attention off of him.

Luckily for Maury, a brand new craze was coming, but little did he know what was in store for his friends and him.

Chapter 2

Maury can't wait for an end
to his attention and fame…
But what's in store will make his tussle with
G.R. Inchworm seem tame!

"Hey Maury, did you hear?" shouted Mikey as he jogged to catch up with his best friend.

Maury turned around to see Mikey wearing a huge smile on his beak. This made Maury smile too. He loved walking to school with his best pal, Mikey. He especially enjoyed the morning walks in the aftermath of saving Christmas for the forest.

Mikey was always good for a joke to deflect the unwanted attention from the paparazzi. Mikey had been Maury's best friend since the first day of preschool and he was even the one who convinced Maury to stand up to the evil bugs in the first place.

In addition to all that, Mikey always had the inside scoop about what was going on around town.

"Hey, Mikey, what's up?" said Maury as his feathered friend caught up with him.

"Did you hear?" asked Mikey.

"Hear what?"

"Hear about what's coming to Forest Noel?" said Mikey.

"Oh no, what's happening now?" said Maury. "Wait, don't tell me. Bill O'Ry Eel wants another interview?"

"Guess again my friend. What I am about to tell you will make you yesterday's news. People will forget about you faster than they forgot about the Mice Bucket Challenge."

"*Thank goodness*," said Maury. "What is it?"

"Facebrook is coming to Forest Noel!" exclaimed Mikey.

"What's Facebrook?"

"Come on. Don't tell me you've never heard of Facebrook! It is the coolest social media site ever. My cousin Ronald lives in Candy Cambridge Forest and they have had Facebrook for months now. He says it is the best thing since sliced bread. And you know how much ducks like bread, so it must be awesome!"

"What does it do?" asked Maury.

"*More like what doesn't it do*," said Mikey. "First you set up a profile, then you add pictures and list all the movies, books and music you like. Then you can add all your friends so they can see your profile. From there, you get to play games, share comments and tell the whole world what you are doing at any given time."

"The whole world already seems to know what I am doing," said Maury. "That's the problem."

"Don't worry," said Mikey. "You know how you always say that we never have time for ourselves anymore? Once all our friends are on Facebrook, it will be so much easier to have a conversation with just us. Plus, everyone will be so busy setting up their Facebrook pages, they will forget all about the *great Maury Chris Moose*. Just give it a try. The whole gang is going to check it out after school today!"

"Okay, I'll go. I guess it can't hurt," said Maury.

Chapter 3

Everyone in Forest Noel wanted to see what
The Facebrook is all about…
Except for Maury whose profile is simply
filled with doubt.

Forest Noel's fifth grade teacher Miss L. Toad had barely finished explaining the night's homework assignment before the entire class rushed out of the classroom. The students had something other than homework on their minds.

"Hurry up, Maury," said Page Ant. "If we wait any longer we will be stuck at the end of the line."

"I am almost ready. I just need to grab my math book from my locker," said Maury.

"You'll have time for math later," said Simon C. Owl. "There is only one grand opening of Facebrook!"

"Okay, let's go."

"Follow me," said Mikey.

The group didn't know exactly where they were supposed to go, but they knew it would not be hard to find. The entire school appeared to have the same plans that they did. A giant crowd was making its way toward Jingle Bell Block. All they had to do was follow the crowd.

"Are we going to Jingle Bell Block?" asked Maury as they approached the area of town that had made them famous.

"Sort of," said Mikey. "The Facebrook is just past the Block. Turns out, when we cleaned up the Block, we did wonders for the surrounding area. The freshly clean land became 5-star property and attracted the attention of a whiz kid inventor who created Facebrook. He saw the sparkling water and decided Forest Noel was the perfect place to expand his company."

"So, you're saying that Facebrook wouldn't be here if not for us?" asked Stoc King Crab.

"*That's right!*" said Mikey.

Just then, the whole gang stopped in their tracks. A large crowd had gathered and they could hardly see the brook or hear the flowing water. It appeared as if the entire school, make that the entire town, had come to see Facebrook's grand opening.

"Look," said Julia. "Even Miss L. Toad is here."

"And there are those rotten twins Eb & Neezer Beetle," said Rob, pointing to the two beetles who had become the group's rivals.

"Remind me to block their friend requests," said Mikey as the group of students filed into the enormous line.

"Wait, you can block someone's friendship on this thing?" asked Maury.

"Yep," said Mikey. "You do not have to let anyone see your profile unless you want them to."

"I hear you can even unfriend someone if you decide to let them be your friend at first, but change your mind later," said Simon.

"That's true," said Mikey. "But I bet it would have to take something terrible to unfriend someone you call a friend."

A teenage fox carrying a stack of electronic chrome tablets approached the group. "Here you go," said the fox.

"What's this?" asked Maury.

"This is the Facebrook eManual," said the fox. "It explains how Facebrook works and lets you set up your profile while you wait in line."

"Sweet! Let's check it out," said Mikey

"First thing the eManual says is to pick a username," said Justine Beaver. "This is the name you will use to get into the site."

"I'm picking *QuackAttack1*," said Mikey.

"Mine will be *SimonSez*," exclaimed Simon.

"I'll pick *PrettyPage*," said Page.

"I'll go with *JustineTime*," said Justine.

"I want *KingCrab23*," said Stoc.

"I'm a *RobStar*," said Rob.

"*JuliaStylez* for me," said Julia.

"How about you Maury?" asked Page.

"Can't I just sign up anonymously?" said Maury

"Leave it to the most popular one in town to want to remain under the radar," said Mikey. "Don't you know everyone is going to want to see your profile?"

"That's what I'm afraid of," said Maury.

"Remember, you don't have to let anyone see your profile if you don't want them to," said Justine.

"Instead of signing up anonymously, how about you sign up as *Anony-moose*?" suggested Mikey.

"Haha. That's pretty good," said Maury.

"Yes, that's perfect," said Simon. "That way you can stay under the radar, but your real friends will know who you are."

By the time the group had finished choosing their usernames, they had progressed to the front of the line. They were now standing smack dab in front of a beautiful brook. The daylight glimmered off the still water, which was so clear it almost looked fake.

Surrounding the brook, the students could see a group of spiders hard at work building webs and constructing a form of netting.

"That must be the world wide web thing my cousin mentioned," said Mikey. "He said the Facebrook runs off the web and the net."

The teenage fox returned and asked if they had picked out usernames. They nodded their heads and handed back the eManuals.

"Now it is time to log on to Facebrook," said the fox. "You simply hop on a log floating in the brook and you will be able to set up your profile. Each log has wireless internet and you can add pictures and all the personal information you want."

One by one, each student stepped onto a log floating by the edge of the bank of water. The logs, each featuring a computer screen, floated into the middle of the brook, cascading on the crystal clear water.

The students eagerly started tapping away on the computer keyboards. Everyone except for Maury, that is.

Still a little leery, Maury decided to poke around the Facebrook website. His parents always told him to read all the details before he submitted any personal information. Maury clicked around, scanning through the set up page and skimming over the legal mumbo jumbo. After watching a quick video tutorial, he spotted a page titled "*Facebrook History.*" Interested in learning about who created Facebrook, he clicked the link.

What happened next nearly knocked Maury off his log. He couldn't believe his eyes when he read, "*Facebrook was invented by...*"

Chapter 4

*Maury thinks Facebrook's creator
is up to no good…
Everyone says to trust him, but Maury
doesn't know if he should.*

Mark Zucker Bug. "Who is Mark Zucker Bug?" Maury thought as he read the name of Facebrook's inventor.

"*Facebrook was created in 2004 by Mark Zucker Bug and his friends in their dorm room at Harbird University,*" read the site's history page. "*Facebrook was initially built only for Harbird students, but because of its immense popularity, it quickly expanded to other schools and towns. Facebrook currently features more than 1 billion users who visit the site on their computers, tablets, PinePhones or any other mobile device.*"

"I knew it!" Maury shouted. "Hey guys, check this out!"

"What is it, Maury?" asked Page. "Did you finish your profile?"

"No. And I will not be giving this site anymore of my information."

"Why not?" asked Simon.

"Facebrook is run by a bug. *That's why*!" said Maury.

"So what?" asked Justine. "Everyone knows about Mark Zucker Bug and how he created Facebrook.

"You guys knew about that? *And you still signed up*? Mikey, did you know?"

"Of course dude. Everyone knows about Mark Zucker Bug. He's a genius. So he's a bug, no big deal."

"No big deal? *NO BIG DEAL*? Have you forgotten about the last bug that tried to invade Forest Noel?"

"That was different," said Stoc. "G.R. Inchworm was a bad bug who was trying to ruin Christmas. Zucker Bug is not like that. You can trust Facebrook, Maury. He's not up to anything."

"All bugs are up to something," said Maury. "I don't trust it. He is probably harvesting all our personal information so he can steal our identities or something."

"Come on, Maury, no one is trying to steal your identity," said Mikey. "Didn't your mom ever tell you not to judge a bug by its cover? Plus, Page is kinda like a bug and she's cool."

"Yes, Maury," said Page. "Not all bugs are bad. Sure, G.R. Inchworm and Eb and Neezer are rotten, but many bugs can actually be trusted."

"I heard Mark Zucker Bug donates a lot of his money to charity," said Julia.

"And Facebrook is doing a lot of good for many people," said Rob. "Thanks to Facebrook, our mom can stay in touch with our giant uncle who lives far away on Sesame Creek."

"I don't know, guys," said Maury. "I know I shouldn't stereotype all bugs as bad, but I still have nightmares about evil bugs invading the forest. It just feels like one of those nightmares is coming to life."

"You can trust us, Maury," said Page. "We wouldn't let you sign up for anything that puts the forest at risk."

"Page is right," said Justine. "We will even help you set up your profile so you know everything is trustworthy."

"Okay, *I guess*," said Maury. "I'll trust you. What do we have to do first?"

"Step number one, pick a profile picture," said Mikey. "You need to pick a picture that really describes who you are. So, maybe you should pick something that says, 'I hate bugs,' haha."

"Very funny," said Maury.

"Mikey is right," said Simon. "You have to pick a great picture. This is what everyone will see when they look at your profile."

"But you can't pick a picture of you by yourself," said Julia. "Everyone will think you don't have any friends."

"I have friends," said Maury. "You guys are my friends."

"We know that," said Rob. "But other animals besides us will see this."

"We are just trying to help you get more likes," said Page.

"More likes?" asked Maury.

"If people think something you put on Facebrook is cool, they can press the like button," said Page. "That shows they like what you posted. And you want to get as many likes as you can."

"Come on guys," said Maury. "I don't care what other animals think. I only care what my friends and family think."

"Well, if you want to be good at Facebrook, you are going to have to start caring," said Mikey.

"I don't know," said Maury.

"Do you trust us?" asked Justine.

"Yes."

"Then let us help," said Justine. "I promise we won't let anything bad happen."

The Forest Noel friends spent the next hour customizing Maury's Facebrook page to perfection. They picked out a great picture of all eight of them from the most recent Christmas party. They showed Maury how to add everyone as friends and how to comment on their other friends' pages so they could all exchange inside jokes.

After adding a bunch of hobbies, likes and silly pictures, the gang was ready to call it a day.

"Thanks a lot, guys," Maury told his friends as they logged off Facebrook. "You were right. This was actually a lot of fun!"

Forest Noel
Facebrook Profiles

Maury C. Moose

Likes

Books - If You Give A Moose A Cookie, Moosebumps, The Three Mooseketeers

Sports Teams - Milwaukee Bucks

Pictures

Friends

Celebrities - Mickey Moose, Billy Noel

Info

TV Shows - Dancer With The Stars, Family Moosers

Games - Duck, Duck, Moose

Movies - Footmoose, Welcome To Mooseport

Hobbies - Pond Hopping, Hanging Out With Friends

Favorite Joke - What do you call a moose who drinks blood? - A Moosequito

Mikey Duck

Likes

Movies - Quack To The Future, The Mighty Ducks

Sports Teams - Anaheim Ducks, Oregon Ducks

Pictures
Friends
Info

Celebrities - James Pond, Michael Quackson

TV Shows - Good Duck Charlie, Duck Dynasty

Hobbies - Flying V's, Swimming, Quacking Jokes

Favorite Joke - What time do ducks wake up?
 - The quack of dawn

Justine Beaver

Likes

Celebrities - Jean Claude Van Dam

Sports Teams - Oregon State Beavers

Pictures
Friends
Info

Movies - My Big Fat Creek Wedding,
Any Documentary About The Hoover Dam

TV Shows - Leave It To Beaver,
Extreme Makeover Dam Edition

Book - The Hunchback Of Notre Dam

Hobbies - Building, Brushing Her Teeth

Favorite Joke - What did the beaver say to the tree?
 - Nice gnawing you

Simon C. Owl

Likes

Games - PineCraft, Guess Hoo

Sports Teams - Atlanta Hawks

Pictures
Friends
Info

Movies - The Fault In Owl Stars

TV Shows - Forest Noel Idol, Yu-G-Owl

Music - The Hoo, Blink 180 Hoo, Hoo Hoo Dolls

Hobbies - Night Flying, Day Napping, Neck Stretching

Favorite Joke - What do you call an owl magician?
- Hoo-dini

Page Ant

Likes

Apps - InsectGram

Sports Teams - Colorado Aval-ants

Pictures
Friends
Info

Celebrities - Barbara StreisAnt

TV Shows - Sponge Bob Square Ants,
Fairly Odd Pair Ants

Movies - Ant Man, Antz

Hobbies - Tunneling, Picnicking, Weight Lifting,
Follow The Leader

Favorite Joke - What do you call an ant that won't go away?
- Perman-Ant

Stoc King Crab

Likes

Celebrities - Tim McClaw, Larry King Crab

Sports Teams - Los Angeles Kings, Sacramento Kings

Pictures
Friends

Music - B.B. King Crab, Nat King Crab Cole

Info

TV Shows - Downton Crabby, Saved By The Shell,
Claw And Order

Hobbies - Digging, Building Sand Castles

Favorite Joke - Why didn't the crab share his food?
- Because he was shellfish

Julia & Rob Birds

Likes

Games - Birds With Friends, Angry Birds

Sports Teams - Arizona Cardinals, Detroit Red Wings

Pictures
Friends

Movies - The Godfeather, Lord Of The Wings

Info

TV Shows - Sesame Tweet, The Big Bird Theory,
Chirp & Dale Rescue Rangers

Shows - Flew Man Group

Music - The Flew Fighters, The Counting Crows

Hobbies - Soaring, Singing In The Morning,
Car Target Practice

Favorite Joke - What do you give a sick bird?
- Tweetment

Eb & Neezer Beetle

Likes

Celebrities - R.L Slime, Bug Hall

Sports Teams - St. Louis Blues, Portland Snail Blazers

Music - N'Stink, Black Eyed Fleas

TV Shows - Bug Meets World, The Biggest Scrooger, Magic School Bugs, Skunk'd, Eel Or No Eel

Movies - The Avengerms, Beetlejuice, A Bug's Life

Hobbies - Bugging Around, Littering

Favorite Joke - Did you hear about the two bed bugs who lived in a mattress?
 - They got married in the spring

Pictures
Friends
Info

Chapter 5

Maybe Facebrook is actually not as bad as Maury feared...
But why exactly is Mikey talking like Black Beard?

"**H**ey, Mikey," Maury said as he met his pal for their morning walk to school.

"ARR, Matey. Top of the morning to ya."

"Huh? Did you hit your head or something?"

"ARR, laddie. Don't ye know what today is?"

"No."

"Shiver me timbers! Everyone knows it be Talk Like a Pirate Day!"

"What's Talk Like a Pirate Day?"

"*Blimey*! Are you pulling me leg? Is this some kind of mutiny? Didn't ye see all the scuttlebutt on Facebrook this morning?"

"No, I haven't been back to the Facebrook since we were all there yesterday," said Maury. "Did you go back already?"

"Aye lad, once ye set up ye Facebrook, you can access it from anywhere on your PinePhone. Only a scallywag wouldn't know that. If you want to stay in the know, ye best be checking ye Facebrook right when ye wake up in the morning. Not doing that is worse than having to walk the plank!"

"If you say so, *cap'n*."

"That's the spirit, matey. Let's set up the Facebrook app on your PinePhone."

Mikey grabbed Maury's phone and downloaded the Facebrook app.

"Buddy, you really have to get with the times," said Mikey. "You hardly have any apps on this thing. There are tons of cool social media sites you can add. There's EweTube, MiceSpace, InsectGram, SnapCat, Pinetrest, LynxIn, TinDeer. Not to mention awesome games like Angry Herds and Clash of the Clams. You need an extreme makeover phone edition."

"I thought you were a pirate," said Maury. "What do pirates know about apps and social media?"

"ARR, ye make a good point. But we best be on our way. Time to weigh anchor and sail off to school. We don't want to play Captain Hooky."

"Right," said Maury. "If we are late, our grades will be in the high Cs!"

"That's the spirit! Yer phone is working already!"

Chapter 6

Facebrook is the talk of the forest and its popularity is growing...
Is it taking over too fast and are the real likes showing?

O ver the next couple of weeks, Forest Noel was engulfed by a tidal wave of Facebrook and many other apps. Now that the animals could get everything on their phones, it seemed like not a minute went by without someone glued to their screen.

Photos were shared, games played, and timelines followed, but some animals were a little *app-rehensive* with all the changes. One moose in particular was not too thrilled with the trend of everyone spending so much time on their phones.

"Mikey? Didn't you hear what I said?" asked Maury.

"Huh?"

"I asked if you wanted to come over to my house tonight."

(5-second delay)

"One second. I just have to finish this game of Birds with Friends. Simon is beating me by 200 points."

"Just forget about it," said Maury. "I can see you are too busy."

(5-second delay)

"Forget about what?"

"Exactly. You are so glued to your phone that you don't even know what we are talking about."

"I am not glued to my phone. I can put it away anytime I want. See."

"I can see you looking at it behind your wing."

"That was just one last peek."

"It is always one last peek. On Monday we spent the whole walk to school in silence because you were looking at Facebrook on your phone the entire time."

"I am just trying to check out everyone's status so I can keep you in the loop," said Mikey. "Speaking of which, what time are you getting to Julia and Rob's tonight?"

"For what?" asked Maury.

"Didn't you see the invitation on Facebrook? Julia and Rob are having a party tonight. Do you even check your Facebrook anymore?"

"I check it...*every now and then*."

"I told you that you have to check it daily, if not more. You are missing a lot. Like the invitation to the party."

"Why didn't they just invite me in person?"

"*Get with the times*. All this goes through Facebrook now. But I am sure they've probably talked about it at school."

"No. They haven't," said Maury. "Everyone hardly even talks at school. Every free moment is spent looking at our phones. I had to keep you from walking into the flag pole at recess the other day because you weren't looking where you were going."

"Thanks. That would have been embarrassing. I never would have heard the end of it on Facebrook."

"Ugh."

"*I know, right?*" said Mikey who was looking at his phone. "Can you imagine the posts? That would have been awful…And speaking of awful!"

"What? Is everything okay?" asked Maury.

"No, everything is not okay. Simon just scored 50 points in our game! There is no way I will come back and win now."

"Ugh," said Maury. "So what time does this party start?"

(5-second delay)

"Umm…one second…sorry, what was the question?"

"Never mind, I will just check Facebrook. See you later."

(5-second delay)

"Uhh…yeah…Facebrook."

Maury checked Facebrook on his phone as he walked home. He had 25 unread messages. Most were friend requests from animals he did not know. He deleted the requests, but thought, "Maybe I should get some new friends. The ones I have don't seem to have much time for me anymore."

He finally got to the invitation to the party at Julia and Rob's.

"Maybe I am being too hard on Mikey," he thought. "I guess times are different with all this new technology and I just have to accept it."

He kept checking his phone as he got home and finished his chores. He convinced his mom to let him go to the party, even on such short notice. He finished his dinner and was on his way to Julia and Rob's.

Along the way, he met Page.

"Hi, Page. Are you excited for the party?"

"Oh hey, Maury," Page said as she stared at her phone. "I guess."

"What's wrong?"

"Oh, nothing," Page said, again not looking up from her phone.

"What do you keep looking at?"

"I'm just checking to see if my Facebrook picture got any more likes."

"What picture?"

"I posted a picture of my new shirt I bought after school and it has only 20 likes."

"*Only 20 likes*? That seems good for something you just posted a few hours ago."

"I guess so, but I have been looking at it all afternoon and I was hoping for at least 30 likes."

"You shouldn't worry so much about the number of likes," said Maury as they arrived at the party. "Our friends probably haven't even seen it yet."

"Seen what?" asked Julia as she opened the door.

"Page posted a new picture on Facebrook," said Maury.

"Oh yeah, I saw that. Cool shirt," said Justine.

"Thanks, did you like it on Facebrook?" asked Page.

"No, but I will if you like the picture I took at recess," said Justine.

"Deal!" said Page.

Maury and Page were the last two to arrive and everyone gathered in Julia and Rob's living room.

"So what should we do?" asked Maury.

(No response)

"Want to watch a movie?" asked Maury.

(Still no response)

"I heard the latest James Pond movie is on TV tonight."

(Still no response)

Maury looked up and found all his friends looking down at their phones. He decided to get out his phone and try something. He clicked the Facebrook app and created an event titled, "*look up*." He scheduled the event to take place in one minute and invited Mikey, Page, Simon, Justine, Stoc, Julia and Rob. Then he sat back and waited.

One by one, his friends' phones vibrated, buzzed and made sounds signifying an alert. His friends pushed buttons on their phones and then got puzzled looks on their faces.

"What's up with this invitation you just sent, Maury?" asked Simon.

"Yeah, what do you mean *look up*?" asked Mikey.

"What do you think it means?" said Maury.

"I don't know. Are you trying to warn us that a meteor is crashing down on us or something?" said Mikey.

"If I was, we'd all be smashed by now," said Maury. "You guys kept ignoring my questions and staring at your phones, so I figured there was only one way to reach you."

"Come on, Maury. It is not that bad," said Justine.

"Yes, it is," said Maury. "We hardly even talk anymore. All we do is chat through Facebrook."

"Don't blame Facebrook," said Mikey. "You spend time on there too."

"You're right," said Maury. "But I think the last time we all actually hung out was when you helped me set up my Facebrook account. If I knew things would get this bad, I never would have done that."

"We are all together right now," said Page.

"You call this *together*?" said Maury. "Sure, we are in the same room, but everyone is so focused on their phones, no one is actually having a real conversation."

"Quit being such a *forest grump*," said Mikey. "I think you are overreacting. Don't be jealous just because we have more Facebrook friends to chat with than you do."

"Jealous? Is that what you think this is all about?"

(5-second delay)

"Umm…sorry…what did you say?" asked Mikey, whose head was once again in his phone.

"Seriously? You are too busy to even have an argument?"

(5-second delay)

"One second," said Mikey. "I just have one more comment to finish."

"How about I finish it for you!" shouted Maury.

With that, Maury stood up and tried to yank Mikey's phone away. Mikey pulled back.

"What are you doing?" asked Mikey, tightening his grip.

"Oh, so now you pay attention," said Maury, pulling on the phone.

Maury yanked so hard that both he and Mikey fell down. The phone slipped out of their tug-of-war and sailed high into the air. Time seemed to stand still as the phone drifted higher and higher. It bounced off the ceiling and crashed into the wall behind them. Maury got up and walked over to pick up the phone. It was shattered into a dozen pieces.

Maury had the room's attention now, but for once he wished that they were back to staring at their phones.

Chapter 7

The phone soared through the air and
landed with a crash…
But it may be more than Mikey's phone that
will end up in the trash.

Maury's eyes were fixed on Mikey's phone, or what remained of it. He did not want to look up because he knew everyone was staring at him. He could feel the heat from Mikey's eyes burning a hole right through him.

"What the heck did you do that for!?!" yelled Mikey.

"I am so sorry. It was an accident. I didn't mean for that to happen."

"Watch out everyone. Hide your phones," said Mikey. "Maury has gone crazy and wants to smash them."

"I didn't *smash* it."

"Looks pretty smashed to me," said Mikey.

"It was an accident. I was just trying to get your attention."

"And you thought destroying my phone was the best way to do that? Why didn't you just say something?"

"I did say something! Everyone was too concerned with what was happening on Facebrook. It was like I wasn't even here."

"I wish you weren't here," said Mikey as he walked past Maury to pick up his phone. "Maybe then my phone wouldn't be in a million pieces."

"Here, let me help you with that," said Maury.

"I think you've done more than enough for one night," said Mikey. "Just leave me alone. Sorry Julia and Rob, but I am out of here. I have to go buy a new phone. Some *so-called* friend just broke my old one."

"Don't leave!" said Julia.

"Yeah, just stay," said Rob. "It's probably too late to buy a new phone tonight anyway."

"My cousin works for Tree-Mobile," said Mikey. "I will see if he can open up the store and get me a new one tonight. Good thing too. I don't think I could go one night without it."

With that, Mikey stormed out of the house.

"Come on guys," said Maury. "That was an accident. You believe me, *right*?"

"Yes…at least I think so…but you were kind of rough with the phone," said Page.

"Just imagine how Mikey feels," said Simon. "Without a phone, he is like, invisible to the world. That thing is his lifeline."

"I was the one who was invisible," said Maury. "Everyone was ignoring me and looking at Facebrook."

"Don't blame this on Facebrook," said Justine.

"Yeah, Facebrook had nothing to do with this," said Stoc.

"Facebrook had everything to do with this. Ever since that dumb thing came into town, there has been nothing but trouble. I don't trust it."

"Just because it was created by a bug doesn't mean it can't be trusted," said Justine. "You have to get over your jealously of its popularity."

"I am not jealous! I just think the bugs are up to something again. They are trying to make us fight and drive us apart. Don't you guys see that?"

"I think you are overreacting," said Simon.

"I'm just trying to protect us so that the bugs don't try to take over the forest again."

"Have you even looked up information on Mark Zucker Bug?" asked Page. "He is not like G.R. Inchworm at all. He seems like a pretty good bug."

"That is just what he wants you to think," said Maury. "You would have to be dumb to fall for that."

That made Page start to cry.

"Maybe it is best if you left too," said Julia.

"Yes, I think you need to go," said Rob.

Equal parts embarrassed and upset, Maury packed up his things and left.

Chapter 8

Maury just knows Facebrook is bad, but no one understands…
To show his friends the truth he decides to take matters into his own hooves.

Before he opened his eyes the next morning, Maury wished that maybe, just maybe, last night's disaster had only been a bad dream. He blinked twice and quickly realized it was not.

He knew he had said some things he would like to take back, but he was just trying to protect his friends. How could they not see what was going on?

But then again, maybe they were right. Maybe Facebrook was not so bad. He grabbed his phone to look up information on Mark Zucker Bug, but before he could do that, he noticed that he had a new Facebrook message.

He clicked on the phone to open the Facebrook app and he could not believe what he saw!

One New Facebrook message: Mikey Duck has unfriended you.

Now Maury's blood was boiling. How could Mikey do that? They had been best friends for years. They saved Forest Noel together. One little accident and they were no longer friends?

Mark Zucker Bug must have something to do with this. That was the only reasonable explanation Maury could think of. That bug is trying to drive a wedge between Maury and his friend. He must have something absolutely terrible planned for Forest Noel.

Whatever Zucker Bug had planned, Maury knew that his friends would not believe him unless he had proof. And if Mikey would not help, Maury would have to do this on his own. He'd have to take matters into his own hooves.

He typed the words *'where is Facebrook headquarters located?'* into the search bar on his phone. He was going to have to find Facebrook and see what they were really up to.

The search results showed the address located in Tall Tree, Crawlifornia.

That was two towns away from Forest Noel. It might take all day to get there, but Maury had to go. He *had* to stop Mark Zucker Bug before that lousy bug brainwashed everyone. Maury quickly got out of bed and brushed his teeth.

"Mom!" he yelled from the front door. "I am going to check out the Facebrook. I might be gone awhile!"

"Okay, honey. Have fun."

Maury plugged the Facebrook address into his phone's GPS and was on his way.

Chapter 9

Maury's journey to Facebrook must go through unknown forests and trees. What's in store for our hero won't come with the greatest of ease.

"**D**umb phone can't do anything right," thought Maury as his GPS was recalculating for the fifth time.

Maury knew that in order to get to Crawlifornia, he could follow the brook where he had first logged on to Facebrook, but because the phone was constantly giving him a new route, he was sure he had missed a turn or two. He had been walking for hours and had never been this far from home.

Just then, he spotted a sign that said "Welcome to Crawlifornia." He knew he must be getting close. At least he hoped he was getting close. Every tree in the forest was starting to look the same and he was not sure which direction was correct. And his phone was not helping much.

Just then, his phone vibrated and slowly turned off. His battery was now dead. Why didn't he think to charge it before he left? How was he supposed to find his way now? A big storm cloud rolled in, making the spooky forest even creepier.

Snnnap!

Maury heard the sound of a tree branch breaking and quickly whipped around to see what was behind him. But nothing was there. All he saw were branches blowing in the wind.

Finally admitting he was lost, he decided he would ask for directions at the next house he saw. About two hundred yards up ahead, he saw the porch light on in front of a large house. He walked over and knocked on the door.

A young-looking 30-something-year-old bug wearing a hoodie, jeans and flip-flops answered the door.

"How may I help you?" asked the bug.

"Sorry to bother you sir, but I think I'm lost. You don't happen to know where the Facebrook headquarters is, do you?"

"You are not from around here are you?" asked the bug.

"No, sir. Sorry to be a bother."

"No bother. I was just doing a little work."

"*Work in a hoodie and flip-flops*," thought Maury. "Does this guy work at the beach or something?"

"Yes, I know where the Facebrook office is," said the bug, interrupting Maury's image of the bug on the beach. "I'd be happy to show you the way. It is actually just around the corner. Follow me."

"Thank you."

"Where are you from?"

"Forest Noel."

"I think I've heard of that. That is the place that is crazy about Christmas, right?"

"Yes, I guess you could say that."

"You must be a pretty big fan of Facebrook to travel all this way."

"Something like that. Umm…I…uhh…just wanted to see what makes it so great!" Maury lied.

"Well, you are in luck. Here we are," said the bug pointing to a huge Redwood tree that had been converted into an office.

"Wow. This place is massive," said Maury.

"Cool, right?" said the bug. "Everything that powers Facebrook happens right here. You should check out the supercomputer, which runs the whole thing. It is pretty impressive. Want me to get someone to show you around?"

"No, thanks. I think I will just take a few pictures from out here and be on my way."

"Suit yourself. While I am here, I might as well just stop inside," said the bug. "Nice meeting you, Maury."

"That's odd," Maury thought as the bug walked off. "I don't remember telling him my name. But I guess I must have."

As the bug walked away, Maury pretended to take pictures with his battery-dead phone. He waited until the bug was out of sight and then he snuck to the back of the giant office. For such an important place, there was not security anywhere to be found.

There must have been over a hundred doors and windows scattered all over the office. "Surely I can find one door or window that is open," Maury thought. "I have to get inside and find, what did the bug call it?–*the supercomputer*. That has to show me what is really going on around here."

Right then Maury spotted exactly what he was looking for, an open window. It was practically inviting him in.

Looking to his left and then to his right, Maury made sure the coast was clear. He decided to accept the invitation and enter into the giant Facebrook headquarters.

Chapter 10

He has made his way into
the belly of the beast…
But what he is about to learn,
Maury doesn't expect in the least.

S queezing in through the narrow window was no small task, especially for someone whose antlers alone are as wide as the opening. Extra careful not to make a sound, Maury scrunched his body just enough to make it into the Facebrook headquarters. It was a tight fit, but he was in.

Once inside, Maury took notice of his surroundings. He appeared to be inside what looked like a break room. A refrigerator covered in magnetic alphabet letters sat on the wall to his right and a sink filled with dirty dishes was on his left. Other than a low purr coming from a half-full water cooler, the room was silent.

He crept to the door, easing it open ever so slightly so he could peek to see if anyone was around. Luckily, the coast was clear. The break room door opened to a long hallway.

Which way to go? *Right or left?*

Maury chose right.

Tip-toeing or rather, tip-hoofing, down the hallway, Maury noticed graffiti covered the walls. "Is that artwork or vandalism?" Maury wondered. "These bugs do not even take care of their own office."

He crept past a door with a red, white and blue pole out front, labeled "The Barbershop" and another labeled "Bike Shop."

"What is this place?"

Out of nowhere, two young bugs on bikes turned the corner up ahead of Maury.

Without time to waste, he ducked into the closest room just before the bugs raced past him down the long hallway. "Bugs on bikes, a barbershop? Is this a business or an amusement park? They have so much fun ruining other animals' lives, they treat work like they are at a fair."

Maury looked around at the room he had ducked into. There was a giant chair with large leather straps on both armrests. Sitting on a creaky old table next to the chair laid half a dozen sharp metal objects. There was a big light bulb that hung down from the center of the ceiling, falling just above the chair. Next to the wall, there was a sink covered in what looked like spit.

"Is this some type of medieval dungeon?"

Seeing there were no more oncoming bikers, the coast was once again clear. Maury closed the door behind him, but did not turn around to read "Dentist Office" printed in large colorful letters.

He kept going down the hallway and saw light coming from an open room up ahead. He could hear commotion coming from the opening. There was chatter mixed with laughter and the clicking of keyboards.

Maury expected to see a room filled with dirty cubicles, but was instead shocked to find a giant open room filled with ping-pong tables, candy machines and video games. There were animals of all shapes and sizes typing away on computers, sitting in beanbag chairs and rocking out to a game of Ants Ants Revolution.

Now Maury was more confused than ever. He had to catch himself from staring. He must keep moving if he was going to find the supercomputer.

Continuing further down the hall, Maury was confronted with another choice to make. The hallway ended, forming a T. He could go left or right. It was a fork in the road. *Literally*. There was a plastic fork on the ground that led to the left. Figuring that led to the cafeteria, Maury went right.

Expecting to find a petting zoo or maybe a dunk tank, Maury was surprised to spot exactly what he was looking for. A large red sign with giant letters spelling, "*KEEP OUT*" was painted on the door.

"This must be it."

He slowly pushed open the door, which swung back and made a loud creaking sound. Figuring everybody was too busy playing ping-pong or getting a haircut, Maury did not bother looking behind him to see if anyone heard the noise.

Stepping into the room, his mouth dropped when he saw the humongous computer screen.

"No wonder they call it the supercomputer," Maury thought as he cautiously approached the glowing monitor. Once he was close enough to touch it, he noticed something odd. There was no mouse or keyboard. Just a screen the size of a movie theater.

The screen was filled with charts and graphs. Random lines of letters and numbers ran up and down and left to right. Maury did not understand what any of it meant.

Initially, Maury's plan was to pull the plug on the supercomputer. He figured that would shut the entire system down. But he could not find any plugs. He could not find any wires or cables. There was nothing to pull.

"How the heck do you turn this thing off? Where is your off switch?" Maury wondered out loud.

Suddenly, the screen became all white and lit up the room. A soft voice asked, "Hello, how may I help you?"

Maury's face turned as white as the screen. He looked around hoping to find that the voice came from someone else, but there was no one else in the room. The voice was coming from the supercomputer.

Frozen in silence, Maury was afraid to speak. Just when he was about to bolt from the room, the computer spoke again.

"I was able to match your face to the profile of Maury Chris Moose. Hi, Maury."

"Uhh…hello. What…I mean…how did you do that?"

"I am programmed to recognize every Facebrook user." The supercomputer then pulled up Maury's profile. "I see you are from Forest Noel. Congratulations."

"Congratulations on what?" asked Maury.

"Forest Noel is currently the most active new community on Facebrook. 99% of all Forest Noel residents have created Facebrook accounts."

"Trust me. I know," said Maury. "*I get the picture.*"

"You want to see pictures?" responded the computer. "Here is the most popular picture currently in Forest Noel."

Right then, the screen flashed to a large image Maury had seen before. The picture was of one-year-old Maury covered in spaghetti. Even worse was what was in the top left corner of the picture.

Posted by Carol C. Moose.

Maury's blood was really boiling now. Not only was the entire forest sucked into the Facebrook trap, but now his mother was too. And to make matters worse, she was posting embarrassing baby pictures of him.

Maury finally had enough. Wires or no wires, he was going to put an end to this. He stormed up to the computer screen. Just as he grabbed it, ready to yank it off the wall, he heard the creaking of the room's door.

Chapter 11

How to take down a wireless computer
that can speak…
That may be the last of Maury's worries
when he hears the door creak.

H iding is nearly impossible in a room that only has a giant, wireless, talking supercomputer on the wall. As the door opened, Maury knew he was busted.

He was ready to run, but stopped when he spotted a familiar face.

"Hey there, Maury," said the bug in the hoodie and flip-flops who had shown him how to get to the Facebrook headquarters.

"Who are you and how do you know my name?" asked Maury.

Before the bug could answer, the supercomputer lit up and said, "Hello, Mark. How may I help you?"

"Mark?" asked Maury. "As in *Mark Zucker Bug*, the creator of Facebrook?"

"That's me."

"But you are so...so...young...and you are wearing flip-flops."

"What did you expect? Some crusty old bug like G.R. Inchworm?"

"Yeah, I guess so."

"Not all bugs are like him. In fact, most of us are pretty good guys, if you take the time to get to know us. Look, Maury, I know why you are here. I know you are not too happy with Facebrook right now."

Knowing it was better to tell the truth, Maury came clean. "Yes, you are right. I got in a fight with my best friend and it's all Facebrook's fault. Things were going just fine before Facebrook showed up in Forest Noel. Now all anyone ever does is look at their computers and phones. I lost my best friend because of this."

"I can see how that would upset you, but destroying the supercomputer is not the way to fix things. And you didn't lose your best friend."

"Yes, I did."

"Computer, will you pull up the profile of Mikey Duck from Forest Noel?" Mark asked.

The computer flashed to Mikey's profile page.

"Did you notice that Mikey posted a picture every Thursday morning?" asked Mark.

"Yes, of course I did. He completely ignored me on our walks to school."

"Did you ever look at what Mikey was posting?"

"No."

"Computer, will you please bring up last Thursday's post from Mikey?"

The computer flashed again and on the screen was an image of Mikey and Maury at Mikey's fifth birthday party. Under the picture was the text: *#TQT* *with my best friend in the whole wide world. Thanks for being my best bud, Maury!*

"What is #TQT?" asked Maury.

"Mikey created what he called Throw Quack Thursday. Every Thursday he would post a picture from when he was little. And every single picture included you. You didn't ever take the time to look, but all those mornings when you thought he was ignoring you, he was really posting pictures of all the great times you two had together."

"Great, but those times are over now. He doesn't want to be my friend anymore."

"I'm not so sure about that. Take a look at the latest update on Mikey's timeline," said Mark.

Mikey Duck is now friends with Maury Chris Moose.

Maury couldn't believe what he was reading. "But…how…I thought he unfriended me. What happened?"

"Why don't you ask him for yourself," said Mark.

Right then, the creaky door slowly opened again.

Chapter 12

The door creaks again and the one who walks in is a familiar face...
Maury and Mikey are all ears as Mark Zucker Bug makes his case.

"**M**ikey? What are you doing here?" asked a stunned Maury when he saw his friend open the door.

"Come on, pal. You know I wouldn't let you have all the fun," said Mikey.

"But how did you find me?" asked Maury

"I followed you. This morning I woke up feeling bad about our fight. I wanted to talk to you about what happened, so I went over to your house. I got there right when you were leaving. When I heard you tell your mom you were going to the Facebrook, I knew you were up to something. I decided to follow you to see what was going on. Unlike you, I recognized Mark Zucker Bug and decided to come clean."

"Mikey told me about your fight," said Mark. "He said you were anti-Facebrook and that you would probably try to shut down the system."

"Uh…well…I don't know if anti-Facebrook is the right way to put it," said Maury. "I just think that everyone is spending too much time on their phones."

"That's not true," said Mikey. "There are just so many awesome things on our phones. Why shouldn't we spend time using them?"

"Okay, so let me get this straight," said Mark. "Mikey, you think Facebrook and other programs on our phones improve the world we live in. And Maury, you think we are spending too much time on our phones and ignoring the things that are really important. Is that right?"

Both Maury and Mikey nodded their heads.

"Before I tell you who is right, let me show you a few things around here," said Mark. "Follow me."

Mark walked out of the room with the supercomputer and took a left down the hall. He walked past the barbershop and the bike repair shop. With Maury and Mikey close behind, he zigged and zagged through hallways inside the enormous office. He did not say a word until the three of them got to the office's waiting room.

A young butterfly receptionist smiled at them as they walked past her desk. Once inside the reception area, Maury and Mikey were in awe of the sheer size of the place. The ceiling was over 50 feet high and a balcony overlooking the second floor shined with colorful artwork and murals.

"This is a little different from G.R. Inchworm's grubby office, huh?" said Mikey.

"For sure," said Maury.

"Come take a look at this wall," Mark said, pointing to a huge black and white wall to the left of the front door. "This is what I call the Wall of Aim. It is a collection of newspaper and website articles from all over the world."

Maury glanced up the wall and spotted a story from the *Crawl Street Journal* titled, "Facebrook Helps Mother Find Her Long Lost Son." Next to that was an article from the *Daily Snail* with the headline, "Soldier Uses Facebrook to See Newborn Son for the First Time."

"The entire wall is decorated with stories showing the power of Facebrook," said Mark. "We have stories of relatives keeping in touch from opposite sides of the world, old animals overcoming depression and young ones falling in love. All thanks to Facebrook. Our company's goal is to make the world a better place. That is our aim. We highlight that goal with the Wall of Aim. I want this wall to remind all employees here that the work they are doing is making a difference. The animals who work here only have to walk into the office to see hundreds of examples of the good their work is doing for others."

"See, Maury? I was right," said Mikey. "That is what you wanted us to learn by seeing this wall, wasn't it, Mark?"

"Not so fast, my feathered friend," said Mark. "We still have a few more stops to make in this office."

Chapter 13

*Maury is amazed with all of the great stories
he was just shown...
And now that he thinks about it, he finds he
has an example of his own.*

Maury could have spent hours staring at the Wall of Aim. He was amazed by how many powerful stories wallpapered the reception area. He never realized that Facebrook was doing so much good for so many animals.

As he followed Mark and Mikey back into the halls of the office, Maury realized he too had an example of how Facebrook can help make connections.

Among the many things Maury did not like about Facebrook was its many notifications. Due to his popularity, he constantly had to delete friend requests from unknown animals. He also received numerous messages from animals who called themselves fans, or even admirers. Since he did not trust the site, Maury assumed the messages were all spam. But every now and then, he would take a quick peek to see what the message said.

One time he received a message from a mother who said her five-year-old son, Danny, wanted to be just like Maury. He was even planning on dressing up as Maury next Halloween. Her son loved Christmas more than anything and was sad when he had to spend the Holidays in the hospital in Forest

Noel. He had a rare disease and would be stuck in the hospital for weeks.

The mom said she understood how busy Maury must be, but it would mean the world to Danny if Maury could come visit and say a quick hello.

Maury was touched by the note. He would have definitely made the visit to the hospital, if the request had come in person, but because he did not trust Facebrook, he figured it was a hoax. He deleted the message.

He thought about Danny and wondered how he was doing. His thoughts were interrupted as Mark walked into a large office with a great view overlooking the city.

"Do either of you know the story of how I came up with the idea for Facebrook?" asked Mark.

"I heard it was to get back at an old girlfriend," said Mikey.

"That is kind of true," said Mark. "A very important part of Facebrook's history does involve my girlfriend, but not many people know the true story. Take a look at this picture on my desk."

Maury and Mikey glanced down at a framed picture of Mark with a lovely ladybug.

"That is a photo of my wife from our wedding," said Mark. "I love this little lady more than anything, but one day I almost lost her. And it was all Facebrook's fault."

Maury and Mikey looked at one another.

"When I first started working on Facebrook, I knew it would be a hit," Mark continued. "I knew I had a great idea that could change the world. But not everyone understood my idea. I had to work non-stop to develop the technology and convince many animals to trust my bright idea. At one point, I was working nearly 20 hours a day. I was super busy and it began to put a strain on my relationship with my girlfriend."

"I was always working and we didn't have much time together. Even when we were together, I was constantly looking at my phone or computer and checking Facebrook. After a while, my girlfriend said she had had enough. She let me know very clearly that she loved me and agreed that Facebrook was a great idea, but it was tearing our relationship apart. She said if things didn't change, she would not be around much longer."

"I didn't want to lose her, so I agreed that things had to change. We created a set of rules that allowed us to spend meaningful time together while also allowing me to help develop Facebrook. The best thing we did was create what we called the 100-Minute Rule. We made an agreement that, no matter how busy I got, we would spend at least 100 minutes together every week. As part of the 100-Minute Rule, there was one condition: no phones and no work."

"When we were together, I had to put Facebrook away. And you know what? Not only did our relationship become better because of the 100-Minute Rule, but so did Facebrook! Facebrook could have burned me out, but the time I disconnected from work and reconnected with what was truly important allowed me to have a clear mind when I went back to work."

"I never would have thought of many of Facebrook's best features if it wasn't for the 100-Minute Rule."

"*Wait*. Let me get this straight," said Mikey. "Mark Zucker Bug, the all-powerful inventor of Facebrook, is telling us that the best thing he ever did was *spend less time on Facebrook*!?!"

"Haha. I bet you didn't expect to hear that," laughed Mark.

"Now I am even more confused," said Maury. "First you show us the great things Facebrook does. Then you show us how it nearly crushed your relationship. Is Facebrook good or bad?"

"Let's make one more stop before I get to that," said Mark.

Chapter 14

*Too much screen time will make any
relationship rocky…
That is when you need more face-to-face
and less walkie-talkie.*

Maury thought about the story Mark had just told. A few minutes ago, he was ready to admit that maybe Facebrook wasn't so bad. But now, the bug who created the darn thing was saying the best decision he made was to spend less time on Facebrook.

The 100-Minute Rule sounded great, so why not make it the 10,000-Minute Rule? If 100 minutes were great, wouldn't 10,000 be better?

Maury remembered back to the party at Julia and Rob's. If they would have had the 100-Minute Rule, he and Mikey never would have fought in the first place. This whole mess would have been avoided.

"Here we are, our final stop," Mark said, interrupting Maury's train of thought.

Mark opened his arms to show Maury and Mikey the giant open room that Maury had walked by earlier. Again, the ping-pong tables, candy machines and video games stood out.

"This is where all the work gets done," said Mark.

"*Work*?" asked Mikey. "This place looks more like a *carnival* than a *cubicle*."

"That is exactly what most visitors think," said Mark. "Everyone sees the beanbag chairs and hears the laughter and assumes that there isn't any work being done. However, I have found that this room allows for more work to get done, not less. Sure we have a relaxed environment, but what else do you hear in addition to laughter and chatter?"

"Typing on keyboards," said Maury.

"Exactly!" said Mark. "Along with a fun place and many toys, you'll find a room full of hard workers who get their jobs done. And you know why?"

"Everyone is on a sugar high?" joked Mikey.

"Close," said Mark. "Open communication. Facebrook has all the best gadgets and gizmos the world has to offer. If we wanted, our employees would never have to speak to one another. They could simply type messages into their phones and never have to look up from their screens. But who would want to do that? Wouldn't you much rather work in a place that combines the wonders of technology with the power of living breathing animals?"

Both Maury and Mikey nodded their heads.

"Earlier, you asked a very important question," said Mark. "You asked if Facebrook and other programs make the world better or if we are all just spending too much time looking at our phones. Well,

I am finally ready to tell you the secret. The answer is…"

"Both!" interrupted Maury.

"What?" said Mikey.

"Both. We are both right," said Maury. "Like we saw on the Wall of Aim, Facebrook is so powerful it can fill a wall with stories of personal connection. But, like the 100-Minute Rule showed, when it gets out of hand, it has the ability to cripple any relationship."

"That is exactly right, Maury," said Mark. "And what do you think our last stop shows us?"

"I'm not too sure," said Maury.

"This giant open office shows us that the question should not be "*is Facebrook or our phone good or bad?*" The question needs to be, "*what is the best way to use them?*" I created Facebrook to help animals understand the world around them. I developed the ultimate communication tool aimed at helping everyone stay in touch with their friends and everything else inside their communities. But it does no good if we are ignoring those same people when they are right in front of us. Why would you connect with someone on the phone, but then ignore them in person?"

"If our heads are always in our phones, the power of Facebrook becomes powerless. By ignoring the person in front of you, you are basically saying that *whatever is happening to me now is not as important as whatever could be happening anywhere else*."

"Facebrook was never meant to take the place of face-to-face interaction. *It was meant to enhance it.* Facebrook should not replace hobbies like sports or reading books. Doing those things and sharing them on Facebrook can help us all learn about what others around us really enjoy. If you give animals a better way to share information, it can change their lives. And that is what we are doing here."

"The `Facebrook office has been so successful because we have found the right mix of technology and personal communication. Do you think you and your friends can do the same thing?"

Chapter 15

*Maury and Mikey got a look into how Facebrook began…
After learning a lesson, they know they must create a game plan.*

Both Maury and Mikey nodded their heads.

"So, let's get back to the real reason you both are here," said Mark. "You had a disagreement and it led to a fight. That is perfectly normal and happens all the time between friends. That is not where you went wrong. Where you went wrong was what you did next. Mikey, what did you do after the fight?"

"Went to my computer and unfriended Maury," said Mikey.

"And Maury, what did you do when you saw that?" asked Mark.

"Came here to destroy Facebrook," said Maury.

"Exactly. Don't you think the better choice would have been to talk to one another in person?"

Both Maury and Mikey nodded their heads.

"Rather than end the friendship at the first sign of trouble, Mikey, you could have explained to Maury that you were upset he busted your phone," said Mark. "And Maury, rather than accuse Facebrook of getting in the way, you could have explained to Mikey why you felt he was spending too much time on his phone."

"Disagreements are going to happen. What is important is how you respond to them. You can allow them to cripple an awesome friendship, or you can use them to make that friendship even stronger."

"I'm sorry, Mikey," said Maury. "I never should have broken your phone."

"And I'm sorry for unfriending you," said Mikey. "I didn't really mean that. You are my best pal."

"That is a great start," said Mark. "And I bet you have some other friends back home who could benefit from learning what you just learned."

"You are right," said Maury. "Thank you for all your help. Come on, Mikey. Let's head home."

"One thing before we go," said Mikey. "I want to take a minute with that candy machine!"

Chapter 16

*Maury and Mikey know exactly what
they need to do next…
They must tell this story to their friends and
do it in person, not by text.*

With a giant bag of candy in hand, Maury and Mikey said bye to Mark and headed for the front door of the Facebrook office. Before leaving, Maury took one last look at the Wall of Aim. It was clear Facebrook made a positive impact on so many lives, including his own.

He had his best friend back.

Maury could not have imagined that he would be thinking such positive things about Facebrook. Just a few hours ago, he had come here to destroy the supercomputer. He had been convinced it was evil. Now he realized that Facebrook was not good or evil. How it was used was what really mattered.

Looking at Mikey scarf down the candy, Maury thought about how good it was to have his friend back. Before he could say anything, Mikey turned to him and said, "I'm sorry for unfriending you." But his mouth was full of gummy bears so it sounded like, "*Om sawerry fahr unfrendling yoot.*"

Maury laughed. "No, I should be the one apologizing. I am sorry for getting mad and breaking your phone."

"No, that was my fault," said Mikey. "I shouldn't have ignored you so much. I was too obsessed with my phone. What's funny is I followed you to

Facebrook's headquarters to prove to you that Facebrook was not bad. I felt I just had to show you it was good. But now I realize it's not really good or bad."

"How we use it is what really matters!" interrupted Maury.

"That is exactly what I was going to say. *Are you a mind reader*? If so, what am I thinking about right now?"

"I am not a mind reader, but I bet you are thinking about that candy."

"*Bingo*!" said Mikey as he popped another wingful of gummy bears into his mouth.

"I knew that was what you were going to say, because I was thinking the same thing. I thought Facebrook cost me my best friend, but now I see it can be used to strengthen my friendships."

"And I thought I would miss something if I wasn't glued to my phone all day long," said Mikey." Now I see that spending too much time on my phone will cause me to miss what's really important."

"How do we get our friends to understand all this?" asked Maury. "I don't think we can bring them all to the Facebrook office and have Mark give them the same tour. We need something that will really hit home with them. What do folks from Forest Noel love more than anything?"

"Christmas presents." said Mikey.

Maury thought about that for a second. "Presents? Mikey, I think you might be on to something."

"Thanks, but I don't think my allowance will be enough to buy everyone gifts."

"No, not *physical presents*, spelled with a 't'. *Presence*, as in being attentive when you are with someone," said Maury. "We need to show them that it is important to be present and not stuck looking at your phone."

"Good idea. We can tell them why it's important to pay attention. Whether online or in person, our attention is the best present we can give."

"And don't forget about Mark's 100-Minute Rule," said Maury. "We should include that somehow."

"For sure. Everyone needs to know how to set limits," said Mikey. "Sounds like we have three good rules: Be present, pay attention and set limits. Now all we have to do is come up with a fancy slogan. Maybe a jingle or something like what companies do to make the idea memorable."

"How about an acronym?" asked Maury.

"You mean like a trapeze artist at the circus?" said Mikey. "Sounds dangerous."

"No, not an *acrobat*. An *acronym*. That is where you take the first letter from each word to form another word. Take the first letters from these three words and let me know what you spell: present, attentive, limits."

"LAP?"

"Close, but rearrange them."

"*ALP*? You think our friends will remember that giant mountain?"

"No, you goofball," said Maury. "*P-A-L*. It spells pal."

"Perfect. We could say that the best way to use social media is to just be a pal," said Mikey. "That is way better than *ALP*."

Chapter 17

*Earlier Maury and Mikey's friendship
looked grim…
Now they are best pals and ready to share
their acronym!*

Maury and Mikey's friends had not heard from them after the two got into that fight at Julia and Rob's – that is, until Maury sent everyone a Facebrook message to meet at Jingle Bell Block the next morning. It seemed odd that Maury was using Facebrook to organize a meet up, so everyone was curious as to what was up.

The confusion increased as Maury and Mikey walked up together, laughing and smiling. It was a major contrast from the other night when the two were at each other's throats.

"It's good to see you guys together," said Simon.

"Yes, we thought you were still fighting," said Page.

"We were, but things have changed since then," said Maury. "We took a little trip and learned something very important."

"I'll explain," said Mikey, clearing his throat and standing up tall as if he was a football coach ready to deliver an important pregame speech. "From the day we arrive on the planet, and blinking, step into the sun. There's more to see than can ever be seen. More to do than can ever be done."

"Aren't those the lyrics to the *Lion King* song?" asked Justine.

"What I am trying to say is we have learned the circle of life," said Mikey, laughing.

"Knock it off and tell them the real story," said Maury.

Maury and Mikey then went on to explain to their friends about their trip to Facebrook. Maury told the story of how he saw Mikey had unfriended him and he stormed off to try to destroy the supercomputer.

The group laughed at how Maury thought the dentist office was a medieval dungeon. The friends were amazed that Maury and Mikey got to meet Mark Zucker Bug. Maury and Mikey went back and forth talking about how cool the Facebrook office was, how Mark showed them the Wall of Aim and gave a history of how Facebrook began.

"I learned that I was wrong," said Maury. "Facebrook is not bad after all."

"And I learned that I was wrong *too*," said Mikey. "Facebrook is not the most important thing in the world."

"What really matters is not how bad or good you think Facebrook is," Maury and Mikey said at the same time. "*It all matters how you use it*."

"So, how should we use it?" asked Page.

"We came up with three important rules," said Mikey.

"Page, remember on the way to Julia and Rob's, when you were sad because your photo didn't have enough likes?" asked Maury.

"Yes."

"When Justine saw you, she complimented your shirt, right?"

"Yes."

"But you didn't take her compliment seriously until she agreed to like the picture on Facebrook," said Maury. "You don't have to judge your value by the number of likes your picture receives. You had a good friend right in front of you letting you know how much she liked your shirt. *That is a real like*."

"We get too caught up on what is happening on our screens that we aren't aware of what is happening right in front of us," said Mikey. "I am just as guilty as anyone. But not anymore, thanks to rule number one: *Be present*. To receive the only likes that matter, we have to be present with those around us."

"Which leads us to rule number two," said Maury. "It's not enough to just be physically present in the room. We have to be there mentally too. Rule number two: *Pay attention*. When someone is talking and we are busy typing away on our phones, we are basically saying, *sure I am here, but what is going on in this room is not as important as something else that is going on in another room*."

"But that doesn't mean we shouldn't use our phones at all," said Mikey. "When used correctly, they are powerful tools that can make any friendship stronger. We just need to be aware of how much we use them."

"Rule number three: *Set limits*," said Maury. "There is a time and a place for us to be on our phones and Facebrook. And there is a time and a place to put them away. If we stick to certain limits, it will make rules one and two that much easier to follow."

"So, there you have all three rules. *Present, attentive and limits*."

"And I've created *an acrobat* to help us all remember them," said Mikey.

"He means *acronym*," Maury chimed in.

"Yes, that too," Mikey continued. "*P-A-L. It spells pal*. The best way to use social media is to be a pal. We could have used the acronym ALP, like that cold mountain, but I thought pal was much better. Speaking of cold, which one of my pals wants to get some ice cream from the new Cold Stone Streamery? I'm buying!"

"You guys go ahead without me," said Maury. "I am going to meet up with a new pal of mine named Danny. I'll catch up with you guys later."

Chapter 18

It may have taken awhile,
but Maury finally came through…
Now there was just one thing left to do.

T he sun was shining, the birds were chirping and Maury could not wait to see Mikey on their walk to school. Usually it was Mikey who had the morning news, but today Maury was the one with the surprise.

"Good morning," said Mikey. "You look particularly chipper."

"I've got big news," said Maury, not wasting any time.

"What? *Is it Talk Like a Viking Day*?"

"Even better."

"*Better than that*? I give up."

Maury pulled out a small white box with a big red bow and handed it to Mikey. "This is for you."

Mikey unwrapped the box to reveal a brand new PinePhone 6 Plus Plus. "Where did you get this?"

"I felt bad about breaking your old one, so I bought you a new one. It's the latest model. I hope you like it."

"It's awesome! But you didn't have to do that," said Mikey, who put the phone in his backpack.

"What are you doing?" asked Maury. "Aren't you going to turn it on and load it up with a bunch of apps?"

"I'll do that later," said Mikey. "Right now I've got more important things to do with *my pal*!"

In today's modern age,
we are surrounded by social media.
It can be helpful and hurtful, and sometimes as
confusing as an encyclopedia.
Building bridges one minute,
the next minute everything shatters.
For something so good and so bad,
how you use it is what truly matters.
Don't ignore those around you
by staring only at your phone.
That is a tough thing to do,
so many of us are prone.
The question is not whether
social media is bad or good,
The question needs to be,
"Are we using it the way that we should?"
It may not be easy,
but social media etiquette can be learned.
Take a lesson from Maury
during the time he felt burned.
When times are tough
and you're running low on morale,
Be like Maury and Mikey
and remember to be a P-A-L!

The End

Made in the USA
Charleston, SC
10 February 2017